Short Tales
of Secret Worlds

I0459211

Deborah L. Alten

Short Tales of Secret Worlds
Copyright, 2015 by Deborah L. Alten

Published by Alten Ink
www.AltenInk.com
ISBN-13: 978-0692495056 (Alten Ink)
ISBN-10: 0692495053

Table of Contents

The Gatekeeper's Prelude

It's a cold morning on Eámanë; a little unusual for this time of year, but not unexpected. Our realm, the last one before Heaven itself, has darkened. Eámanë has inched closer to the Ninth Gate, better known as Black Hole #32206445.

Recently, a reddish mist has emerged from the Ninth Gate, which could open and swallow us whole. It hasn't yet, but it is a tale worth writing about. After all, this is what I do: observe, protect (those who let us), and to write down the history of each planet, world, and universe.

I am the Gatekeeper, one of 300. The scrolls of every world, even yours, is at the tip of my pen.

Of course, if we should sink into the Ninth Gate, all the tales we've written are lost. Therefore, I shall leave some of the scrolls with you. Keep them safe; these tales of secret worlds. Some say, they might even contain the history of an alternative world that never was. We dare to differ.

Where Dragons Live
The First Tale

"There are no more dragons, sir." Gha'enna caressed the innkeeper's face with the back of her sun-bronzed fingers. "Perhaps you'd be so kind as to pour me a pint of ale, slice me a piece of bread, and spare me a bowl of warm stew." Her lips were close to his as her nimble fingers unfastened the buttons of his disheveled shirt. "Here's me last few pence."

He trembled at the mere touch of her skin on his. "Keep it." His voice a quiver.

She threw a bloody tether onto a table and brushed off the crumbs. Her green eyes fixed on the innkeeper. Never trust a man who … Well … never trust a man.

The stale bread, dipped in warm stew, satisfied her hunger … for the moment. She washed it down with badly-brewed ale.

Then, as she cleared her throat, Gha'enna slapped her hand onto the coiled-up tether.

"Something stuck in your throat, my lady?" The innkeeper's forehead furrowed.

Gha'enna grinned nervously, struggling to take a few breaths and one hard swallow.

"I smell …" The innkeeper grabbed a knife, "a dragon."

"I told you, sir." Gha'enna straightened up. There are no more dragons. You would call a lady a liar?"

He stood frozen, mesmerized, as moonlight danced through her long red hair. And her smile rendered him powerless. There was nothing he could do but stare. The innkeeper believed every word that fell from her lips.

"Forgive me. Ne'er would I call a lady by such a name."

Then from the corner of the dimly-lit tavern, a figure rose from the darkness. "Indeed." His voice was like a rushing wind and deeply disturbed Gha'enna.

She jumped at the first sound of it. And though it seemed familiar, she placed no memory to it.

A heavy black and bloodstained cloak covered him. His face, not visible. The innkeeper cowered behind the bar. The stranger crept closer. "You would not call a lady a liar?" He turned to Gha'enna. "She is no lady, Innkeeper."

Gha'enna held tight the tether. She backed away from them both.

The man adjusted his cloak as he made his way around broken chairs and spilt ale, toward her. "Where *have* the dragons gone, my lady?"

"I have slain them all."

"All?"

"Have your eyes seen them? Where and when?"

The tether in her hand stiffened. She caressed her throat; an attempt to dislodge something she could not quite swallow. Her eyes searched for his, to no avail. She coughed as she gasped for that extra breath of air.

"Innkeeper, has she blinded you with her beauty? Her words, or perhaps the sweetness of her lips has held you captive." His gloved hand appeared from beneath his cloak. Chainmail rattled. "She makes fools of men, and her paths lead to spirits of the dead. At night she stands at forbidden doors. Do you not see the dragon?"

"I only see her," said the innkeeper.

Gha'enna giggled. Then unexpectedly she flung the tether across the room. It coiled around the innkeeper's neck and tossed him high above the tables. An horrific, wicked growl tore the roof off the tavern. One blood-curdling scream and the innkeeper's feet dropped with a splat into a puddle of his own blood. The other parts of his shredded body, burned, then swallowed or trickled like bloody crumbs onto the dirt floor.

The knight unsheathed his sword against the fury of dragon fire, but Gha'enna's red wings carried her away before he could plunge it into her cold heart.

The Warrior

"You never called him King?" Ráh wrapped the silk scarlet cord around her wrist. She dipped a cotton towel into dirty water and rinsed the blood off the warrior's face.

"We did … call him King. He said it did not suit him." The warrior sat up. "In my world, when the last king passed, Jesha took the throne. We just let it be. Strange really, though it seemed right."

War ravaged the city just outside the arched windows. Ráh's ear hugged the wall. "Listen." In the distance, lowly chants of a thousand voices echoed from the ocean's shore. "Jesha …" She turned to the warrior. "They say he was born a slave."

"Thus the scars on his back." The warrior eased to his feet. Smells of spilt fuel filtered through shattered glass. His eyes widened as another airship fell from the sky. "This city will fall." With every blast the blade of his sword rattled amongst the rubble. "It doesn't seem that—"

"Your weapons could destroy us?" She picked up his sword. "How will this defeat an army of flying machines, and submarines, and ships that walk on water?"

"Yours is a strange land, Ráh. But we do not mean to fight with weapons."

Her brows crunched, her head tilted. And for a moment they forgot the war outside. They forgot they were enemies. She was not someone a man should fall for, but he kissed her nonetheless.

Suddenly, a knock. He jumped, sword in hand. The knocks grew louder, more insistent, as surging chants of ancient warriors rumbled like thunder.

"Open the door!" A rough, garish voice drilled through the portal.

The warrior tilted his head and raised his eyebrows. "A patron, Ráh?"

"A palace guard." She hung her head in shame. "Go to the roof of the dark tower."

"Come with me. This world is passing. Jesha will lead us. He is a good king."

"But he is no king at all."

"The sun stood still for him … a full day, Ráh. That is no ordinary man." The warrior checked the portal then walked toward the spiral staircase. "Leave the scarlet cord on the windowsill. No harm will come to you. Wait for sunrise."

A barrage of micro-missiles battered the door. The cogs turned, rattled, but held together. Then through the bronze portal a shell burst through, its red tentacles targeting Ráh's heart. The warrior leaped from the staircase and with his blade deflected the stray shot. The pounding continued till the door spun off its hinges. Ráh ran for cover. She searched for the warrior through the glittering dust of basalt debris But he was gone.

More guards, escorting Prince Jericho, forced their way into Ráh's home. Ráh knew them all. The prince offered her half his kingdom if she would but hand over the spy. She never did. But she did leave her scarlet cord on the windowsill.

At sunrise, she heard Jesha's people march around the city. They were a strange and peculiar people; their voices like death rays, their weapons mere songs. Each note pierced the instruments of every flying machine. Ships sank, subs imploded. And the shrill choruses from Jesha's army melted the black steel-curtained wall of the city.

Steam spewed from every corner. Gaslights ceased. When Ráh walked through the ruins, she found the warrior waiting at the iron gate. He wrapped the scarlet cord around her wrist and embraced her.

"Perhaps we should call him King now?" Ráh's eyes followed Jesha's victorious parade into her city.

"No. He is only the messenger."

Broken
The Third Tale

"Recall."

"Excuse me?" Terrin yanked out the last of the crossed-up wires inside a metal skull and flung them on a silver plate with the rest of the android's broken parts: hands, feet, eyes, hair, and artificial skin tissue. She pulled the rusty lever of the old furnace and cast the skull into the fire. "What did you say?"

Ries took the wiring from the plate and carefully untangled it. "Recall. Section 22 is now called Recall."

"Does it matter? It's still all about the broken parts." She picked up another skull from the pile of shrapnel and held it up to the light for Ries to see. "Look at this crack. Its creator obviously missed it; too fine to detect when this unit was first released into the new world."

"Or perhaps he did it on purpose."

"Why would he do that?"

"I don't know." Ries took the dysfunctional unit from Terrin's slender fingers. "Maybe its defect was its advantage. And we failed to see it as such." He walked slowly around the underground lab looking for components to reassemble this unit.

Terrin wiped the soot off her forehead and continued her work. "It's broken, Ries. Useless. It never functioned the right way, therefore it lost its purpose."

Ries shook his head and sighed. "Or found it. Do we know its name?"

"No, it's one of the lower units. Wait, 316 is engraved on the collar. Meant for menial tasks: clean house, wash clothes, feed children. Do I need to go on?" Terrin's eyes followed the young man's every move now. "What you got there?"

"Its recall papers." Ries adjusted his glasses. "Says it failed to adjust … never accomplished any of its tasks. But—"

"But what?"

"It learned to love."

"It what?" Terrin took off her oil-stained apron. "Give me that." Her brown eyes scanned over the paper, line by line. Her fingers traced each word as if not to miss one, or miss the meaning of one, or misread one. She read quietly.

Ries began pacing and more than once tried to snatch the papers away from her. "Well, what else does it say?"

"It took care of the children. That, by the way, doesn't mean love, Ries." She blew a stray strand of brown hair out of her vision view. "On more than one occasion it was caught showing the children how to take care of themselves. That's just laziness."

"The 316's had laziness programmed into their wiring? Now that's a defect."

Terrin crunched her eyebrows.

Ries picked up a discarded torso and carefully placed it inside a body bag. It clanged around with other spare parts. "Take a look around you, Terrin. We create AI, then we destroy it because it hasn't done what we thought it should have done. Maybe it's us. We don't see, or even understand, what its creator had planned for it."

"I blame its creator then." Terrin winked. She seemed satisfied with her revelation.

Just then the horizontal doors of the lab opened above them. Light from the outside world streamed through the open shaft. A shrill horn sounded as bodies of metal, some with human-like features, cascaded down the chute. The doors closed leaving disheveled piles of brokenness.

Terrin took a deep breath. "I'll take the heads, you separate the legs." She reached for the first unit. "Another 316. Almost human—blue eyes, warm skin." Terrin's hands trembled slightly. She turned to Ries. "Want to read its recall papers first?"

Ries zipped up the body bag. "Yes, yes I do."

Beneath the Blithe of Silver Moonlight
The Fourth Tale

As mist descended upon Elmsley village, a young man, wrapped within a heavy cloak, snuck up on the grey-stone cottage at the edge of the frozen forest. He was drawn to the lights of burning candles flickering through foggy windows. Backing up against the cold, moss-covered stones a soft snarl escaped his lips. Breath became one with the mist.

A wooden bench in front of the cottage labored beneath a layer of fresh snow. There, he thought, he would end it all; just one sturdy stab to the heart with his silver dagger. Surely the gods of winter would not frown upon him now. Surely no other had ever bore such a burden as his.

From the forest, a wolf's daunting howl echoed through the mist. Should he obey its cry? He peeked through the window. Was she there? She was. Could she save him one last time?

The young maiden spun her yarn from the spindle. Her ailing mother, sheltered beneath a cloak much like his, rocked back and forth upon a feeble rocking chair. Yarn spun around her bones of decrepit hands. Trickles of blood entwined. She endured her pain. Together, mother and daughter sang a haunting song as a child lay on a bed of straw and a newborn babe slept peacefully in a cradle.

Without realizing, he began to sing along. His scarred hands blotting bloody imprints onto the window.

Mother looked up as flames from the soot-coated fireplace reflected in the hollow of her eyes. Her bony fingers pointed to the window. The young maiden looked over her shoulder. Her blue eyes met his. For a fleeting moment he felt peace. But the cry of the wolf persisted. As did his hunger. He turned away and set his sights on the silver moon casting ominous shadows from brittle branches.

"Decide, my love, which path you should go." Hers was the still small voice within a storm.

He turned. For a time, as he watched his children in undisturbed sleep, he thought of fighting the hunger. But it growled violently inside of him. Then, under the blithe of moonlight, flesh and veins churned, bones crackled, and blood meshed with matted hair—no longer human.

By the time he crept into their warm cottage there seemed nothing left of his humanity. He licked empty a bowl of steaming soup as she emerged from behind her spindle. Sharp teeth, dripping with spittle vile, sniffed close to the maiden's fair face. She stood her ground between him and their children. It was then that he backed away, almost prostrating before her. A tear fell through his closed eyes. Macabre shadows of wolf and tortured man danced amongst the flames.

And she sang once more that haunting song. Each note to soothe a broken soul.

Again, as evening's shadow falls,
We gather in these hallowed walls;
And vesper hymn and vesper prayer
Rise mingling on the holy air.

May struggling hearts that seek release
Here find the rest of God's own peace;
And, strengthened here by hymn and prayer,
Lay down the burden and the care.

O God, our Light, to Thee we bow;
Within all shadows standest Thou;
Give deeper calm than night can bring;
Give sweeter songs than lips can sing.

Life's tumult we must meet again;
We cannot at the shrine remain;
But in the spirit's secret cell
May hymn and prayer for ever dwell.

The howl of the wolf, in the gloom of the forest, loudened. But her voice had reached his soul as it had done so many nights before. The pounding of his heart waned, the hunger subsided. He surrendered to the Song. Next to him she lay and gently stroked his back, which rose and fell beneath her tender touch.

Covering his body with a tattered, bloodstained blanket, the Song remained upon her trembling lips. She wept.

Then, slowly she withdrew the silver dagger from his heart. With fading breaths, he drifted into eternal sleep … into the arms of redemption.

Again, As Evening Shadows Fall, 1859. Lyrics by Samuel Longfellow. Music by Angelus, St. Alkmund. (public domain)

Off Guard
The Fifth Tale

For two weeks a steady rain had battered the ancient forest. Malatthias was cold and hungry, the weight of his armor tiresome. By the time the second moon rose he wore but his tattered shirt and bloodstained pants, his sword still sheathed. A thick cloak covered him and part of his horse, Mayllyn.

Suddenly, a snarl came from above. He looked up. She was dark, beautiful, and for the moment the dis-enchanted knight remained mesmerized. *Look away.* He could not speak.

She slowly descended toward him. "I am Kteress." It was more like a hiss than a woman's voice.

Mayllyn stood straight up on her hind legs, plung-ing the knight into the thistles and thorns. He scrambled to his feet but Kteress was on him within a blink of an eye. Her claws dug around and into his throat.

For a fleeting moment when her gaze turned else-where, he heard the distant voice of his dead father. "She makes men weak with lust; turns their hearts with her deceptive beauty. Men must look away. Set their minds on better things, worthy things: whatever is true, whatever is noble, right, pure and admirable." But the pounding of the rain washed away his father's words.

She parted her red lips, dripping with raindrops like honey. Sharp white teeth gleamed by subtle moonlight. She bit into the flesh of his neck, slow and deep. He moaned. It was his blood she hungered for.

"Become like me," she whispered. "Immortal."

The stare of her black eyes brought him to his knees. He struggled to breathe as he felt life fading.

Kteress licked her lips as if to taste the death of this knight till he cried out to the heavens, "Grant me Your strength just one more time." A surging force reached into the innermost part of his being. He unsheathed his sword and thrust it through her cold heart.

She flailed while her claws cut deep into Malatthias' face—through his temple, over his left eye, beneath the bridge of his nose, down his right cheek. From his bleeding throat a horrific scream of pain and anger erupted.

But Malatthias did not let go of his sword. Her high-pitched screech vibrated into his ears as she thrashed about. Yet she could not free herself from his blade till he pulled it out, little by little. Her body convulsed in the mud. As thunder roared, the ground beneath swallowed her whole.

Malatthias collapsed onto this back, losing his sword to the rising puddles of water which splashed and mingled with his blood. He closed his eyes and groaned. Rain fell harder. Someone called his name, over and over again.

When he opened his eyes, many breaths later, the rain had eased and a shadowy figure appeared from within the mist.

"Father?"

"Where is your armor, Son?"

A Life Between
The Sixth Tale

Skahl cleared his throat and licked the blood from his cracked lips. For three days, smoke had hindered his breaths. Sulfur packed his nostrils. And when he swallowed the muddied dregs of water from the pouch, a taste of putrid chemicals crept into his mouth.

His last meal was the bounty from a tree with withering branches but soft golden fruit. Its bark was bruised; leaves brown, desperately holding onto life. A small pool of murky water puddled beneath it. *Blood*? He wasn't sure. It would explain the taste of decay.

His journey continued into a fractured land—vast and dry; frozen in twilight, haunted by half-light. There *was* one bright star shining directly onto a stone manger in a lonely cave—a place Skahl could not reach. The more he traveled toward it the farther away it slipped. But he continued to walk in its direction. He didn't know why. Perhaps he was losing his mind. Perhaps he was dreaming.

Ashes of burning rubber fell like snow, scalding his skin. What lonely place had he landed in? Once in a while he heard a child cry. Then a whisper like a cool spray of water. "Daddy." Skahl would quicken his pace, twist his body to the right, then left, but saw nothing. Soon the cry faded and the emptiness was not only around him, it was in him.

He fell asleep. Not a peaceful sleep but a nightmare of hissing voices; hands and arms sweeping across his chest and pulling him into an orange river. The river spewed liquid fire and mud boiled on its banks. He surrendered—he'd been here awake.

Slowly he sank, his body disintegrating; flesh melting off his bones. Pain was different here, always on the brink of death, but never quite reaching a final breath.

Skahl woke, still in this place, this infinite, dry, abandoned place. Again, sulfur thickened the walls of his nostrils. He coughed, licked his lips and scrambled to his feet. Off in the distance, he heard someone hammering a nail into a tree. Every time the hammer fell a horrid shriek of pain echoed through the empty space between them.

A warm trickle of blood dripped from Skahl's nose, his head felt like lead, his ears rung. Skin flaked off his hands when he tried to clean the blood. Again the hammer fell. He cupped his hands over his ears and stumbled forward, slamming into the trunk of a tree. It moaned.

No. It can't be. Skahl cursed the tree that had fed him. He kicked it, then yanked its fruit. "Back where I started?"

A wreath of thorns and thistles reflected onto the murky puddle. Washing his hands in its bloody waters he whispered, "Someone died here."

Once more he heard the cries of a child. "Daddy." The voice seemed familiar. But he ran. He ran toward that one bright star. He ran from the child who kept calling for him, disturbing his soul. He ran for three days, till he fell into the cracks of the thirsty land, passing out from exhaustion. And when he woke, his hand grazed the bark of a tree. He tried to scream, to cry, but only dry heaves came. He gagged, rolled over, pounding the earth with bleeding hands. And the cries of a child echoed louder.

If only he could reach the light and find what—or who—it shone upon. If only he could breathe … or die. If only he could find the child.

The ground shook beneath him as a voice screamed out. "Daddy. Daddy, fight. You're not dead yet!"

One more chance … He reached out to the light. "Save me!"

The Soldier
The Seventh Tale

"Make certain the tower is locked, and the priest still breathes. Then get out. The portal closes within the hour." Gad retracted his battle-torn wings as he gave J'than his orders.

The soldier nodded and reached for his M16 Mach 1.

"Don't bother." Gad shook his head. "Your weapons cannot go through the portal. However, the Watcher's sword rests atop the tower. The Nephilim left it there. For the priest I suppose."

J'than frowned. He clenched his fists which wrapped his body armor around him from head to foot. Taking a breath, he stepped through the portal. But on the other side, hydrogen sulfide infiltrated his lungs. He coughed till he managed to activate his oxygen pack.

This was the unfamiliar world. The one men tried not to believe in. J'than located the tower. Horrid cries, voices within the walls—exhausted voices—screamed for mercy.

J'than stood both in awe and fear of the tower. Yellowy-brown mortar oozed between the bricks, spitting out drops of red. *Blood.* "Still fresh." Vines and roots choked the craggy stones, strangling life from each layer. The roots dripped with pungent liquid. And a constant banging of broken bones clanged through living walls.

The soldier ignored the pleas. His job was to secure the tower. "Flight." J'than's voice-command equipped his body armor with wings—F22-Raptor particles. He fortified the tower, every lock he bolted, every crack and hole he sealed.

He found the sword. It was longer than he expected and heavier. With sword in hand he walked into a cold cave. There he saw the priest. A pouch of coins dangled from his tattered belt. His pale blue hand clutched a bloody sword. Red veins lined his black eyes. And an open wound, unable to heal, scarred his neck. "Where is your sign? Let me see your forehead."

J'than's grip on his sword tightened. "No sign."

"No sign! No pass!" Then, with unexpected velocity, the priest charged toward J'than.

They clashed midair. Sword upon sword, resonating through cavern walls.

"Who are you?" J'than hollered as iron ignited.

"You can't kill me. I'm already dead. We could fight for eternity."

"You wouldn't last. Just tell me who you are and I might let you live." J'than backed away, though his sword pointed at the priest's face.

"I betrayed Him, you know. With a kiss no less." Saliva trickled from the priest's lips.

"This I knew," J'than replied, "I needed to hear you confess it." The soldier slashed the pouch with his sword which scattered the silver coins. "Your reward!"

The priest scrambled to gather his coins but J'than grabbed him by the scruff of his neck and lifted him off the ground. "Scelestus. Traitor! You truly are lost." He threw the priest's body onto the parched ground. Thump! Bones rattled and broke.

The priest staggered to his feet. "Go. Perdition waits. Why you travel here is none of my concern. You will not return."

"I came to make sure you had not found a way out."

The priest stroked the wound on his neck. "Did they kill Him?"

"Who?"

"The One who sang all worlds into being."

J'than walked toward the closing portal. "Yes, they did. But three days later he rose. I didn't believe it myself until I saw you. I'm guessing it's why they sent me."

The portal closed. The soldier was gone. Lava bubbled across the parched land. The gnashing of teeth grew louder. The ancient tree appeared and a noose slithered down. The priest hung himself … again. Three days later, breath returned to him. He sighed. *Eternity* … "This is Hell."

Je'thal, Leviathan, and the Gatekeeper
The Eight Tale

"Why can't we enter?"

The Gatekeeper knelt beside young Prince Je'thal. "Behind that door lies a dark path, cold and endless. Not many men find their way home."

"The way to the Dark River?"

"It *is*." The Gatekeeper hammered a sconce into the crevice to hang his torch. "But the door is heavy, not easily opened."

"Let me try?"

"But why, my prince? It is certain death." The light of the torch reflected in the Gatekeeper's eyes. "Of course, if you should make it to the river's bank, near the edge of the sinking forest, you would find the last of the Healing Trees. Sometimes their weeping is heard across the land."

"Why do they weep?"

"The people are dying. Disease is spreading and we cannot reach the medicine of the branches until *he* sleeps.

"He?"

"Leviathan." The Gatekeeper covered his head

with the hood of his tattered cloak. "Difficult to pass this monster. He sees in the dark. His fangs drip with the poison of his tongue. And his tentacles will wrap you as easy as a spider does her prey."

"How did it get in the river?" Je'thal's eyes widened.

"No one knows. It belongs to the sea, but he *does* have wings. Though no one has seen it in flight." The Gatekeeper lit another torch. Shadows shifted. "Leviathan has crushed strong men, tore them, limb … by … limb."

Whoosh.

A chilling breeze whistled through the tunnel. Then a thud on the door. The prince gasped. "Their ghosts?" Je'thal pressed closer against the warrior. "We should never open that door."

The Gatekeeper nodded. "One day, someone must. We need the medicine of the Healing Trees— just a few branches. It has been ten years since the last knight came back alive, but only because he failed. He turned back when he saw Leviathan."

"Were you the last knight?"

The Gatekeeper hung his head and sighed.

"DO NOT ENTER": words scratched upon the old door. Moss grew over its frame. Spiderwebs clung from rusty hinges. King Je'thal removed the torch from its iron sconce. His hands trembled. Nevertheless, he opened the door. Muddy paths of the cave, littered with the skulls of men and beast, led to the Dark River.

He crept through the ghostly cavern. Shadows danced over human remains as the flame passed over them. Dead men whispered, "Turn … back … now." Dangling vines slithered from an earthy ceiling.

Je'thal battled his way to the mouth of the watery cave. He took a breath and dove into the icy waters. Firefly squid lit his way. Then suddenly they scattered. A low growl, like a dragon sleeping, stirred the waters.

He swam up, past the sleeping monster; dagger be-tween his teeth, sword in hand. He eyed the branches of the Healing Trees dipping into the water where moon-beams rippled. He reached out of the water taking hold of the nearest branch. Snap!

The sea serpent woke. Instantly, Leviathan whipped his tentacles around Je'thal who twisted within its hold. Then unexpected … freedom.

Je'thal kicked through whirlwind-like waters back to the mouth of the cave. He heard the thunderous moans of land separating; crashing down into the river. The rush of the water pushed him forward till it flung him onto the muddy floor of the cave. The Healing Trees came roaring down and settled with a thud. Water surged over him and then receded, closing the entrance to the Dark River.

Something sparkled between the rattled branches. Je'thal reached for it—the Gatekeeper's sword; the old Gatekeeper attached, in one piece and still breathing.

When Worlds Collide
The Ninth Tale

The structure to the right of Para'Mal Hospital, the Amelia Earhart Wing, is marked for demolition. If all goes well the old wing will implode. It's taken months—strategically placing explosives, gutting, and removing all glass windows.

Detonation is set for 7:30 A.M. on July 2nd—today. But early this morning a crew member reported hearing a voice from within the doomed building. I'm assuming it's me.

For months I've been a witness to this disassembling. I thought to stop it, but nobody hears me. I'm disturbingly sure they can't see me either. After all their gutting, not a thing changes in my world. The structure we occupy is staying intact. Perhaps I'm seeing things. This, of course, would mean I'm also hearing things. I need rest. Is there time to figure this out? My daughter is scheduled for surgery.

July 2nd, 7:00 A.M., the surgical team stands ready to perform the operation on my girl. They found two large sacs of poison on her lungs.

"She's been breathing some toxic dust," they say.

For the last three months she's worked here as a nurse on the nightshift. More than once she reported seeing clouds of dust appear in certain rooms; windows rattling and walls shifting. None of this she could prove because it all settled back to normal by the time they came to investigate. Understandably, she stopped giving reports.

Then there is that young man. When she first tried to talk to him, he couldn't hear her until the windows began to shake. On occasion, where he appears, some windows are missing altogether. That's when she can hear him better, but still from afar, like he isn't even in this world. And apparently he isn't. Somehow our worlds, or time itself, has overlapped. Is it possible, if the building is coming down in their world, it will come down in ours?

It's 7:15 A.M., and I see the young man trying to stop detonation.

"I've seen them!" he's yelling.

They think he's crazy. I think I'm crazy. Sometimes I see the empty, gutted hallways but it returns just as quickly—the doors, beds and medical personal. One minute I'm alone, the next I'm bumping into Dr. Know-It-All, the one who suggests I calm down.

"You are having illusions, you are hearing things," he says.

Tell me something I don't know.

My daughter is frantically calling for me. Blood is dripping from her nose and she's coughing up a powdery kind of substance.

The young man appears in her room. "There's not enough time," he's screaming. "Leave the building. It's all coming down."

She can hardly breathe and the staff is strapping her down to the gurney. "Calm down!" they yell.

Her face is turning fiery red and she continues to gasp for air.

"Enough!" I charge into her room, release the leather straps, and throw my coat over her.

The digital clock above her bed flashes 7:20 A.M. We run—her arm over my shoulder, my arm around her waist. I drag her down a flight of stairs to the lobby door. We make a clean escape and scramble for the exclusion zone.

Seven thirty, July 2nd: I can hear the countdown. And then ... detonation.

We never saw the young man again; never heard voices, or had visions of gutted buildings, since the Amelia Earhart wing came down. No one knows how. It just imploded. My daughter and I know. Two worlds collided, a wrinkle in time occurred. But we remain silent. What really happened that morning, when thousands of lives changed, will have no place in our history books.

Morning Star
The Tenth Tale

Morning Star cleaned the blood off his wings in the cool waters of Blue River. His eyes fixated on his re-flection. "I am magnificent," he whispered. "The seal of perfection."

Morning Star's battered wings, torn near the veins, began to heal. There was nothing, or so he thought, that could harm him.

"Truly, I am invincible." He retracted his massive wings, which vanished the shadows into the evening mist. "Truly, I am almighty."

The ground beneath him shook. The sky rumbled. A still, small voice rose from the ripples of the Blue. "I AM who you want to be. You ask for sorrow."

"No. I ask nothing. I am filled with true wisdom. I possess beauty every creature desires. I shall sit on your throne." Morning Star burst from the chains of gravity and flew to the heights of Black Mountain. He stood on the edge of Black's most infamous cliffs and screamed across the heavens. "I am god of every world. There is no other! Who will follow me?"

Morning Star gathered them, those who would trade light for darkness, near the ancient trees of Green Forest. They were beautiful, each one shone with the brilliance of their maker. But with every step toward Green Forest, their hearts blackened, their eyes dimmed, their garments reflecting something they were not familiar with—death.

"Do not turn back. Do not be fooled. The Light is weak. We will have dominion over all His creation." Morning Star sauntered through the masses of his followers. "You are the strong, you are the chosen. Surely death will never find you. All wisdom and knowledge is yours. You have no need to serve Him, because you will be like Him ... and even better."

A loud cry of defiance shattered the peace like shards of glass. "Hail Morning Star!" they cried out with thunderous resound.

On the other side of the Blue River, Captain soothed his battle-torn wings in the cool waters. Their strength returned. He washed his hands, splashed his face, and let the drops stream over the open wounds of his back. "Fools," he whispered.

He heard their cries, their alliance to Morning Star. His eyes shone with a brilliance which turned heads away. "Too pure," they said.

If he had looked upon his own reflection he would have known he was magnificent. But he never looked. If he had heard the whispers of the created ones he would have known he was stunning, full of wisdom, courageous and powerful. But he never listened.

He carried out the Creator's commands, knowing that war was coming.

In the days to follow, Morning Star and his armies crashed through the barrier to where Creator dwelled. But they never reached him as Captain and his host of armed forces intercepted.

Many years this battle raged. Both sides with great casualties. Morning Star carried the essence of his dead into his wings becoming more powerful. But many times he stayed on the sidelines as it pleased him to watch them die for him.

"See, Captain, they worship me."

Captain took the time to address him. "Ironic, I would say, … it is your splendor corrupting your wisdom; your beauty deceiving your heart."

Morning Star laughed. "Brother, come with me and I will give you the keys to His kingdom. I will rule and you shall be elevated above all others."

"I am not your brother, Morning Star." Captain drew his sword. "And this is your last day in Creator's realm." He took a step closer and smiled. "I reject your proposal."

The battle between Morning Star and Captain escalated beyond all the others. Wings were slashed, bones were broken, flesh was pierced. There seemed no end till Captain whispered this one thing: "The name of Creator is
in me."

Morning Star grabbed his heart. "No!" he bellowed.

Captain thrust his sword through Morning Star's heart. He took the last beat, though not the life.

Morning Star's light left his being and Captain cast him out; down to the blue planet and even below it. One by one those who pledged their loyalty to Morning Star fell from the heavenly places to the darkness below. And the weight of their sins kept them shackled.

Light of the Worlds
The Last Tale

In all the realms of every universe the news spread faster than light: the Blue Planet— the Dark World—was chosen to receive Creator's Son.

Cynda sank into the mounds of ram skins and woolen mantles strewn about her silvery throne. "Why the Dark World?" Her fingers ran through playful strands of her golden hair. She eyed the messenger. "There's blood on their hands. Anger rules their hearts. Hatred fills their eyes. Will they know Creator's Son? Or even recognize him?"

"They might not." Gad retracted his wings, shaking off a trail of stardust. His blue eyes scanned beyond the crystal craters outside the arched windows.

"Tell Creator we are at His service."

"That is greatly appreciated. I am afraid, however, that the Son will have to complete this assignment on his own."

Cynda shook her head and sighed. "What is the assignment?"

"To save them."

"From themselves?"

"Mostly." Gad prepared his wings for flight. "And from Satha. He's darkened their minds. Together they have made quite a mess of things." He looked over his shoulders toward her. "You have done well to keep your distance, though once or twice their iron ships have touched your shadowlands."

"We have seen them. But they could not see us."

"Their eyes cannot see divine things." Gad opened his wings slowly till they stretched beyond the mercury walls. "Your light will soon be needed."

"I am ready."

Suddenly the space around her was void of his presence. Cynda never liked when messengers departed. She worried about them. "Sons and daughters of men ignore the messengers. They do not know Light and worship the darkness." She spoke in whispers to herself. "And what will they call him? Is there a name suitable and would they be worthy to even speak it?"

"Cynda!" Her baby sister, Cusha, tumbled into the room, her dress draggling sparks of white light. She toppled over limestone floors before jumping onto Cynda's lap. "Have you heard? Have you heard? He is going to save them after all."

"Yes, I've heard. Though it appears they do not think they need saving, he will do it nonetheless."

Cynda brushed the slivers of light from her sister's hair and hugged her.

"Is Cynda all right?"

"Cynda is fine." She straightened Cusha's flowing white dress. "The Light is coming to the Dark World. That is good news, Cusha."

When Gad returned many days later, he swept Cynda into his arms and flew her into the darkest part of the universe. Not one of her kind had ever been that close to Creator's Blue Planet.

Gad left her there. "Do not fear," he told her. "This is what you were created for."

She danced with nighttime breezes. Twirled in the vastness of space till the light within her burnt brighter and hotter than it had ever done before. It scared her to think she might not survive. But fear subsided when she remembered Gad's words: "Do not fear. This is what you were created for."

Beneath her light lay a child wrapped in swaddling cloths. *Creator's Son in a stone trough.* She caressed his cheeks. He stirred within her warm glow. It saddened her to see him in such obscurity and poverty.

But she lit the path for kings who sought him, for shepherds who believed in him. All was not lost for the generations of the Blue Planet. Cynda burnt bright till all who searched for him found him. "Here is your King," she whispered. "What will you do with him?"

Other Titles by Deborah L. Alten

1. Mrs. Shackles: The Flash Fiction Chronicles
2. The *Self-ish* Writer (with Julie A. Cave)

www.ingramcontent.com/pod-product-compliance
Lightning Source LLC
Chambersburg PA
CBHW030328130626
46554CB00011B/1087

9 780692 495056